The Big Fib

by **Tim Hamilton**

I Like to Read®

Holiday House / New York

I LIKE TO READ is a registered trademark of Holiday House, Inc.

Copyright © 2014 by Tim Hamilton
All Rights Reserved
HOLIDAY HOUSE is registered in the U.S. Patent and Trademark Office.
Printed and Bound in November 2013 at Tien Wah Press, Johor Bahru, Johor, Malaysia.
The artwork was created with pen and ink,
watercolors, and digital tools.
www.holidayhouse.com
First Edition
1 3 5 7 9 10 8 6 4 2

Library of Congress Cataloging-in-Publication Data
Hamilton, Tim.
The big fib / by Tim Hamilton. — First edition.
pages cm. — (I like to read)
Summary: After playing with Miss Finn's discarded boxes and
making a mess, her young neighbors first lie about their misdeed
and then make things right.
ISBN 978-0-8234-2939-4 (hardcover)
[1. Honesty—Fiction. 2. Behavior—Fiction. 3. Boxes—Fiction.
4. Imagination—Fiction.]
I. Title.
PZ7.H1826588Big 2014
[E]—dc23
2013009705

For my wife, Jean,
who knows that the truth
is mightier than the fib

One day
Miss Finn got rid of
a lot of boxes.

We took some boxes
and made a train.

Then we played a train game.
We went far, far, far.

We took two more boxes
and made race cars.

Then we played
a race car game.
We went fast, fast, fast.

We took more
and made a jet.

We went up, up, up.

Miss Finn came out.
"Who made this mess?"
she said.

"The wind,"
I said.
But that was
a big fib.

"The wind?" said Miss Finn.
My big fib got bigger.
"It was a big wind," I said.

Miss Finn picked up the boxes.

She was slow,
slow, slow.

"We will pick up the boxes,"
I said. "The wind didn't
make the mess.
We did."

"I'm glad you told the truth,"
said Miss Finn.
Then she gave us milk
and cookies.

"Let's play a game,"
said Miss Finn.
"I am queen.
You are my knights.
And we are friends."

"You don't have to play
that we are friends,"
I said. "That is real."

You will like these too!

Dinosaurs Don't, Dinosaurs Do
by Steve Björkman

Fish Had a Wish by Michael Garland
Kirkus Reviews Best Children's Books list
and Top 25 Children's Books list

I Said, "Bed!" by Bruce Degen

I Will Try by Marilyn Janovitz

Look! by Ted Lewin

Pete Won't Eat by Emily Arnold McCully

See Me Run by Paul Meisel
A Theodor Seuss Geisel Award Honor Book

See more I Like to Read books.
Go to www.holidayhouse.com/I-Like-to-Read.